THE SEVEN PEBBLES

ROHIT

Dedicated to the beautiful nature!!

Contents

Foreword

Humans like any other substance on planet earth endures various environments and circumstances. The inner self might never change!!

Preface

The book steers through inferences drawn between similarities in integral structures of substances when exposed to varied environments.

Acknowledgements

Travelling is the best form of learning!! Sincere gratitude to all associated in travel industry. Thus making learning fundamentals of life easier and effective!!

CHAPTER ONE

Childhood

Jade was born in Rocher de Monaco in the year 1996 to an affluent couple and grew up seeing all the luxury around her. The Rocky promontory overlooked the Mediterranean and formed the oldest part of Monaco. She woke up each morning with the susurration of waves which could be heard from the window pane of her bedroom.

As a ritual, Jade used to visit the shore every Sunday morning, pick up the most beautiful pebble her eyes could catch and secretly kept it in the drawer of her study table. She would then clean them and choose the most colourful pebble. When the collection grew substantial, in her next visit to the shore, she used to disperse the remaining pebbles back to the Mediterranean. The ritual continued till Jade started her college with Geography as the main core subject. Her father and mother knew the secret bag she was hiding for all these years and finally they asked Jade to disclose the secret behind the collection. Jade told her parents about her Sunday morning ritual and explained that after following such a meticulous process over the years, she is finally left with seven pebbles. She continued expressing her ideology and reasonings and selection criteria as if this was the most important aspect of her life. Surprisingly, when she opened the secret bag to show the collection to her parents.

The pebbles each unique in appearance looked nothing less than a collection of jewels. With her heartbeat growing louder, she exclaimed that this was the collection of her lifetime. Amused at hearing the secret, her parents smiled gently and hugged their daughter. "So what do we do now with these seven jewels" said her father. Jade took a deep breath and told that she wants to travel the world and distribute the pebbles at different environments worldwide and devote her life in understanding the world through these pebbles. Her parents were happy to hear their daughters' ambition and extended all the moral support as a parental gesture.

CHAPTER TWO

The Ambition

On her twentieth birthday, Jade waved a goodbye to her parents and started off her journey. She made seven slips with seven continents of the world mentioned in the slips and placed the slips in the magical velvet bag of pebbles. She decided to pick one of the pebbles and one of the slips to commence the project.

The first pick of the slip revealed Africa written on it and the pebble was a round grey-bluish one. She boarded the flight from Paris to Cape town in South Africa. On landing at Cape town she headed for Clifton Beach where she intended to place the first pebble. Clifton Beach was one gorgeous white sand beach with a landscape of beautiful mountains and granite boulders. It was a mesmerising scenic beauty at first glance. Jade checked into a beach resort, where she planned her next few days to plant the first pebble. Without wasting any time, she opened the tool kit and drilled a small hole in the first pebble and embedded geo location sensor and a small solar powered accelerometer into it. The next few days went in to identify a place on the beach to disperse the pebble. And then was the difficult part. It was really hard, for Jade to now say goodbye to the first pebble after she immersed it into the Clifton Beach Sea Shore. She took many photographs of the pebble as well as the location where it was immersed. Her eyes were filled with tears as she was so much attached to her seven pebbles.

She left for the Cape Town Airport and as a next step, chose another slip and pebble. The slip had Oceania written on it and it was a sharp-edged reddish pebble. She booked the tickets to reach Melbourne to accomplish the next Goal of her ambition. Landing at Melbourne was smooth and weather was a bit windy. She was so desperate in achieving the next goal, that she first went to St Kilda Beach and there she planted her second Pebble. The ambition continued for Asia, Antarctica, North America, South America and in her return leg back to Monaco in Europe. She joyfully hugged her parents on arrival and talked out so many things about her adventure lasting three months, touching upon all the continents and leaving behind her precious jewels at each continent. "Now what" exclaimed her father. Jade laughing loudly told her father that now its time to start her Sunday morning ritual again till she finds better jewels than previous ones. Saying this, she retired to her room and after a short nap she opened her laptop to observe the technical parameters of all the seven pebbles.

CHAPTER THREE

Observance

Without fail, Jade used to check the data recorded by all the seven pebbles. She tried a lot but could not observe any findings or changes the pebbles were undergoing. Days passed, months passed and years passed, Jade got busy with other important aspects of her life. As years passed, it was a long time Jade had a look at the pebbles data. Time flew and Jade was married. Her family grew bigger in size and had three sons. Years passed and each of his son were blessed with two kids each. In no time, Jade realised that it was time for her seventieth birthday. Her six grand children asked her if they could gift her something special. Jade in a feeble voice requested them if each one of them could travel to a location she would share and find the pebbles and gift it to her. It would answer many curious things of past. They promised her and by travelling through the modern supersonic travel flights brought the pebbles back to Jade. The pebbles had sustained fifty long years. The pebbles no longer looked the same as they used to fifty years back. Jade also observed that each of the pebble had reduced a lot in dimensions just like her over the years. Jade finalised her geography thesis with a note, that she observed seven pebbles underwent exposure to all walks of life on earth and never disintegrated even in the harshest of the conditions. Throughout the exposure the seven pebbles retained their unique appearance from the granular inside. Every substance on Earth gets exposed to distinct environments. The substances will continue remain unique come what may and might never disintegrate from the inside.

On her next birthday, Jade received Nobel prize in Geography and Environmental Sciences for her devotion in researching impact of time on substances of earth.